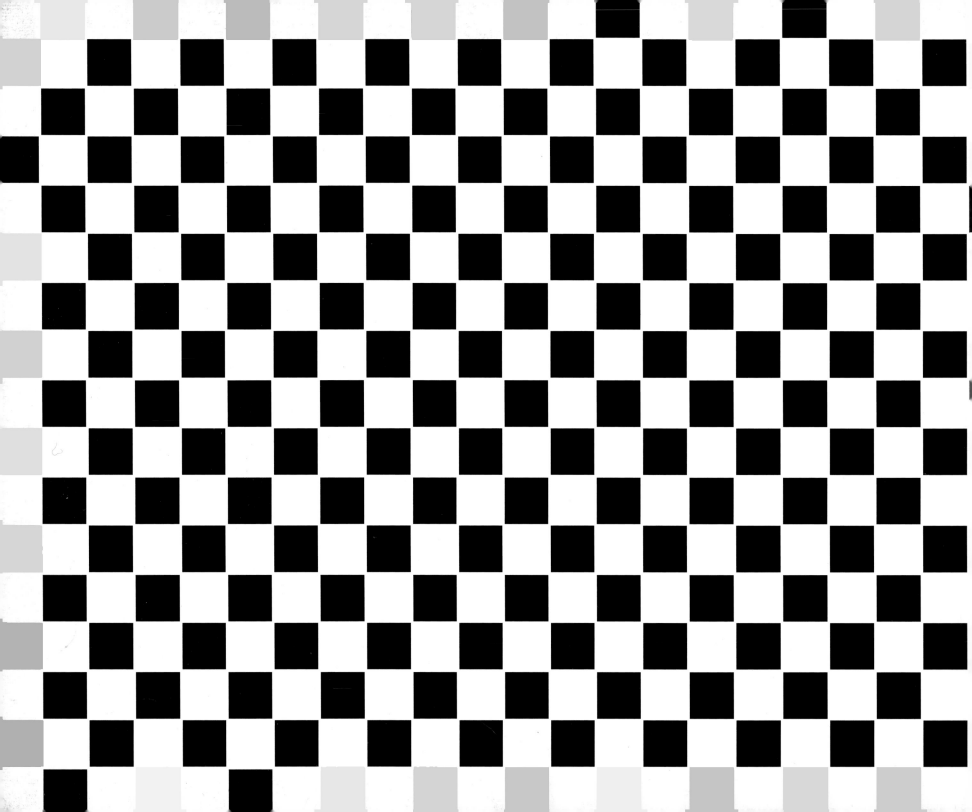

It's Me, Marva!

A STORY ABOUT COLOR & OPTICAL ILLUSIONS

by Marjorie Priceman

ALFRED A. KNOPF   NEW YORK

to my Mother
& to ROY G. BIV

THIS IS A BORZOI BOOK PUBLISHED BY ALFRED A. KNOPF

Copyright © 2001 by Marjorie Priceman

www.randomhouse.com/kids

Library of Congress Cataloging-in-Publication Data
Priceman, Marjorie.
It's me, Marva! / Marjorie Priceman.
p. cm.
Summary: Mishaps involving color and optical illusions befall Marva as a result of her new invention, the Ketch-o-matic.
ISBN 0-679-88993-0 (trade)
ISBN 0-679-98993-5 (lib. bdg.)
(1. Color—Fiction. 2. Optical illusions—Fiction. 3. Visual perception—Fiction.) I. Title.

PZ7.P932 It 2001
(Fic)—dc21

00-030213

KNOPF, BORZOI BOOKS, and the colophon are registered trademarks of Random House, Inc.

Printed in the United States of America
May 2001
10 9 8 7 6 5 4 3 2 1
First Edition

Marva was in the kitchen
putting the finishing touches
on her new invention,
the Ketch-o-matic.
   She tightened a screw.
   She twisted a widget.
   She flicked the power switch.
      The machine *hummed*,

then *shimmied*,

      then—

SPLAT!

Ketchup on the floor.
Ketchup on the cat.
Ketchup on her head.

Marva thought she looked
good with red hair. Very hip.
Very Hollywood. As she rinsed
off, Marva imagined life as a
redhead.

But when she was done, her hair was

ORANGE!

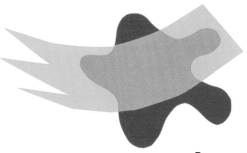

Because:

Red (ketchup)

+ yellow (hair)

= orange (hair).

Marva decided to consult a professional. She went to Betty's House of Beauty—in disguise.

"It's ME, Marva," she whispered. Then she took off her scarf.

"Orange hair!" said Betty. "Very festive. Very Florida."

"Can you make it red?" said Marva.

Betty got right to work. First she poured bleach on Marva's hair to remove all the color. Then she counted to twenty. While Betty counted, Marva admired the new wallpaper.

"1, 2, 3, 4, 5,
6, 7, 8, 9, 10, 11, 12, 13, 14, 15,
16, 17, 18, 19, 20,

DONE!" said Betty.

Marva turned back to the mirror. "Betty!" she cried. "I have the MEASLES!"

To see what Marva saw:
Stare at the polka dots for
20 seconds under a bright light.
Try not to blink. Then look at
Marva's face.

"You look fine to me," said Betty while she poured red dye on Marva's white hair.

Then Betty rinsed and dried Marva's hair. "Uh-oh," she said.

"Oh, NO!" said Marva. Her hair was not red.

"Very posh," said Betty.

"Very pink!" screamed Marva.

Because:

Red (dye)

+ white (hair)

= pink (hair).

Blue SALE!

Leaving the House of Beauty, Marva spied a lovely vase in a gift shop window. It was the perfect shade of blue to accent her living room.

She went into the store. She took the vase to the counter to pay for it.

But she was hypnotized by the salesman's necktie and forgot what she was doing. She forgot who she was and where she was.

When the telephone rang, Marva snapped back to her senses.

Stare at the necktie for
10 seconds. Are you getting
sleepy? Now meow like a
kitten. . . . Just kidding!

Pleased with her purchase, Marva continued on her way. But the snickers of some children reminded her that her hair was still pink.

Marva went to the Wishy-Washy Laundromat to meditate on the problem.

She put her new blue jeans in the washing machine. Then she threw in her yellow scarf and her red shirt. She poured in some soap.

She waited. The hum of the dryers and the churning of the washers soothed Marva. Her mind wandered to faraway places. She forgot about her hair. She forgot about her laundry—until the buzzer on the washing machine buzzed.

Marva looked at her clothes.
She screamed. Her yellow scarf
was  **green!**
Her red shirt was
PURPLE!

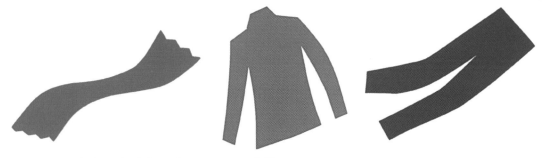

Hari Panjabi, who owned the
Wishy-Washy, shook his head sadly.
"There is a lesson to be learned
from this," he said. "The lesson is
this: Never throw new blue jeans in
the wash with a red shirt and a
yellow scarf."

Because:

Blue (jeans)

+ yellow (scarf)

= green (scarf),

and

blue (jeans)

+ red (shirt)

= purple (shirt).

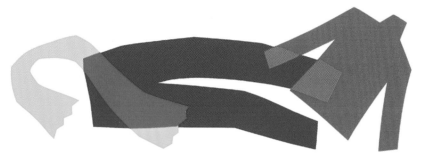

"That's good advice," said Marva. Then she said, "Have you seen my blue vase? I had it when I came in and now I can't find it."

They looked around the waiting area. They looked under the tables and inside the dryers.

"There it is!" said Hari. "It's right on top of that washing machine!"

To find Marva's vase:
Stare at the orange wall for
20 seconds under a bright light.
Try not to blink. Then look on top of the
washing machine on the next page.

When Marva got home, she put
her new blue vase on a table in the
living room.

She was shocked! Her blue vase
didn't look blue. It looked
PURPLE!

Marva took the vase into the kitchen. Now her vase was **BLUE** again!

Marva ran back and forth between the living room and the kitchen, and each time the same thing happened. Living room—purple! Kitchen—blue!

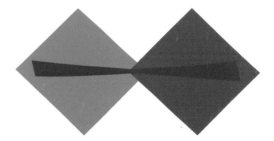

Because:

A color will appear to change when placed against different-colored backgrounds.

All this excitement was giving Marva an appetite. She was in the mood for Jell-O, but all she had were the same old flavors.

Then Marva had an idea. She would create fantastic new Jell-O flavors!

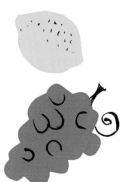

She poured a box of lemon and a box of grape in one bowl. Then she combined cherry and lime in another bowl. And in the third bowl, blueberry and orange.

Marva was imagining life as a Jell-O tycoon when the timer rang. She flipped the Jell-O molds one by one.

Voilà! The lemon-grape was the color of mud.

Voilà! The cherry-lime looked like dryer lint.

Voilà! The blueberry-orange was asphalt gray.

Because:
Yellow and purple, red and green, and blue and orange are complementary, or opposite, colors. When opposite colors are mixed, the result is brown or gray.

Marva glanced at the clock. The inventors' club was meeting tonight. She changed her clothes and went to Elsa's house.

Elsa answered the door in a smart new dress.

"What a pretty dress," said Marva. "I *love* cats."

"Cats?" said Elsa. "These are SAILBOATS!"

Look carefully at Elsa's dress. You may see both cats and sailboats.

Marva took a seat in the living room while Elsa went to get refreshments. Stan was about to demonstrate his invention, the Dogbrella.

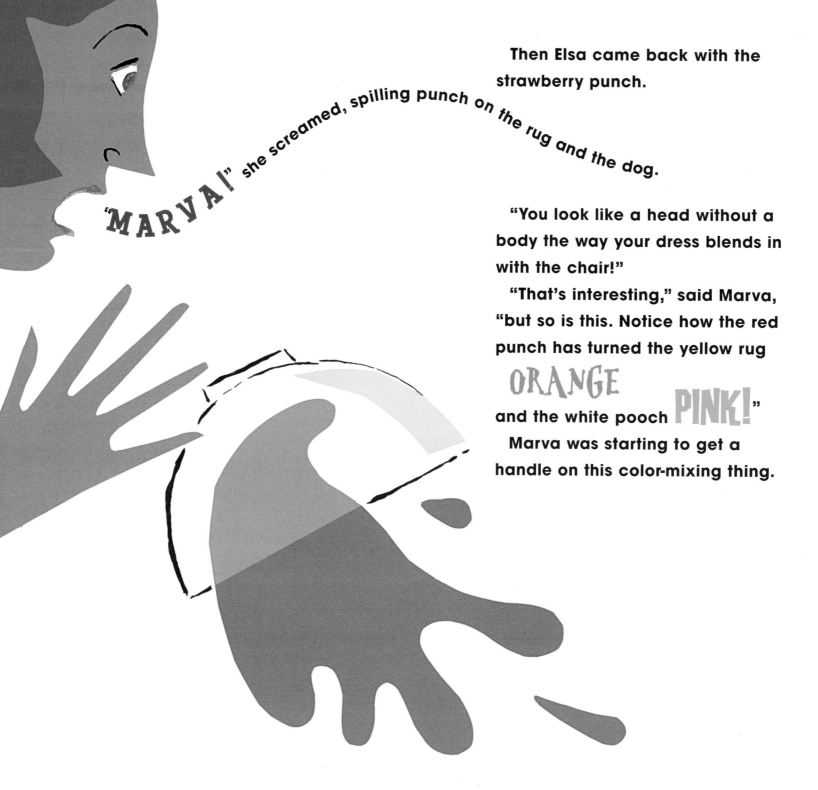

Then Elsa came back with the strawberry punch.

"**MARVA!**" she screamed, spilling punch on the rug and the dog.

To see what Elsa saw
Look at the next page
from across the room

"You look like a head without a body the way your dress blends in with the chair!"

"That's interesting," said Marva, "but so is this. Notice how the red punch has turned the yellow rug **ORANGE** and the white pooch **PINK!**"

Marva was starting to get a handle on this color-mixing thing.

One month later, or maybe two, Marva was rollerblading in the park when she crashed into a jogger.

"Excuse me, miss." It was Hari Panjabi.

"It's ME, Marva!" said Marva.

"Marva! I didn't recognize you... with PURPLE hair!"

"I'm still working on it," said Marva.

"It's very new," said Hari. "Very YOU."

Marva smiled. Hari smiled back.
"Look!" said Marva. "Through
the trees—a rainbow!"

"Beautiful," said Hari. (But he was
looking at Marva.)
At that moment, it was clear there
was something special between
them.

To see how this story ends:
Stare at the trees between Marva and Hari
for 20 seconds. Try not to blink.
Then look at the page to the right.

color mixing

RED, BLUE, and YELLOW are called primary colors. They cannot be made by combining any other colors. But by mixing RED, BLUE, and YELLOW in varying amounts, every color in the universe can be made.

When you mix two primary colors, the result is a secondary color. The secondary colors are ORANGE, GREEN, and PURPLE.

Tertiary colors are those in between primary and secondary colors on the color wheel. Some examples are BLUE-GREEN and RED-ORANGE.

Adding WHITE to a color makes it lighter, and the new color is called a tint. (PINK is a tint of RED.)

Adding BLACK to a color makes it darker, and the new color is called a shade. (MAROON is a shade of RED.)

Colors that are opposite each other on the color wheel are called complementary colors. Mixing complementary colors neutralizes them and results in brown or gray.

optical mixing

When small bits of two colors are next to each other, as in a checkerboard or stripe pattern, your eye will mix the two colors together, resulting in a third color. How well this works depends on how small the bits of color are and from what distance they are viewed.

This is exactly what happens in the printing process. If you look at a magazine picture under a magnifying glass, you will see it is really made up of thousands of tiny dots of color. The pixels on a computer screen create pictures in much the same way.

vibration or motion

When you look at a pattern like the salesman's necktie, your eyes may have trouble focusing on both the close-set lines and the wide-set lines at the same time. The places where the wavy lines are close together are more difficult to focus on and may appear blurry. This shifting in and out of focus combined with the wavy pattern of the tie may be perceived by your eyes as motion.

A similar phenomenon happens when opposite colors (like RED and GREEN) are placed side by side. Because your eye sees color in wavelengths and RED and GREEN have very different wavelengths, your eye has trouble processing both colors at the same time. The result is a buzzing effect where the two colors meet.

afterimage

In your eyes there is a receptor on the retina for each color you see. When you stare at one color for an extended time, the receptor in your eye for that color eventually becomes desensitized, or fatigued. When you relax your eyes by looking at a white surface, your eyes respond by "seeing" the same shape you were staring at. However, you see it in the exact *opposite* color, since your eyes rely on the receptor that is least tired. Stare at this weird wedge for 20 seconds. Then look down at the plate and see what's for dinner!

color change

How we see a color depends a lot on what other colors are around it. The brighter and more intense colors are least likely to change. These are called hues and are the reddest reds, greenest greens, bluest blues, etc. But a lot of in-between colors such as the BLUE-PURPLE of Marva's vase can appear to change dramatically. Keep in mind that BLUE plus RED makes PURPLE. So, in reality, Marva's vase is some combination of red and blue. Placing the blue-purple vase on a pure BLUE background, as in the first picture, will cause the vase to look less BLUE by comparison and therefore more PURPLE. In the second picture, the pure RED of the background overwhelms the RED in the vase color, making the vase seem more BLUE by comparison.

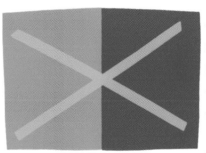